Willie's Game Day Rules

Story © 2014 by Sherri Graves Smith

Requests for permission to make copies of any part of the work should
be submitted online at info@mascotbooks.com or mailed to Mascot
Books, 560 Herndon Parkway #120, Herndon, VA 20170.

The indicia featured in this book are registered trademarks of the Kansas
State University.

PRW0514A

Printed in the United States

ISBN-13: 9781620866542
ISBN-10: 1620866544

www.mascotbooks.com

WILLIE'S
GAME DAY RULES

Sherri Graves Smith

Illustrated by Damon Danielson

Hello, I'm Willie the Wildcat, and welcome to K-State's court.
I'm here to give you some simple rules on how to be a very good sport!

When you're standing in a line,
it is best to take your time.

Patience is something you will learn,
when you kindly wait your turn.

If you step on someone's feet
on the way to your seat,
"excuse me" or "I'm sorry" will do
when asking someone to pardon you.

Remember, it is thoughtful to say,
"you're forgiven" or "that's okay."

Remember, it is nice to share with others,
not just your sisters or brothers.

If someone does something kind,
a simple "thank you" will do just fine.

If a player makes a mistake,
it's never a reason to act with hate.

It is great to love our team,
but to our rivals, don't be mean.

It is okay to celebrate and cheer with fans,
just be close to your parents in the stands.

It is even okay to jump around,
just do not knock someone down.

If the ref's call is not for us,
it's not right to shout and fuss.

If the ref's call puts us in first place,
let's not rub it in our opponent's face.

Even though players guard and block
to keep others from making shots,
be sure to watch them interact carefully.
Players help each other and try not to bully.

When you watch the halftime fun,
clap for them when they're done.

If our team comes out on top,
it is great to cheer a lot!
But a sore winner, you should never be.
Winning is not a reason to be mean.

Remember, before you leave the game,
clean the spot from where you came.

If you're five or seventeen,
you can always help someone in need.

If you want to see good
sportsmanship and have
some time to wait,
at the end of the game, look
down court to watch the
teams congratulate.

Thanks for listening on how to be a good sport
by minding manners at our court.

Be sure to come right on back! Where we'll
cheer and shout "Go Wildcats!"

Check out these other *Game Day* titles from Sherri Graves Smith and Mascot Books:

-Albert and Alberta's Game Day Rules (Florida)

-Big Al's Game Day Rules (Alabama)

-Mike the Tiger's Game Day Rules (LSU)

-Buzz's Game Day Rules (Georgia Tech)

-Cimarron's Game Day Rules (Florida State)

-Hairy Dawg's Game Day Rules (Georgia)

-Rameses' Game Day Rules (North Carolina)

-Aubie's Game Day Rules (Auburn)

-Smokey's Game Day Rules (Tennessee)

-Cocky's Game Day Rules (South Carolina)

-Tiger's Game Day Rules (Clemson)

-Reveille's Game Day Rules (Texas A&M)

-Bully's Game Day Rules (Mississippi State)

-Nittany Lion's Game Day Rules (Penn State)

-Go Blue's Game Day Rules (Michigan)

-Big Red's Game Day Rules (Arkansas)

-Truman's Game Day Rules (Missouri)

-Blue Devil's Game Day Rules (Duke)

-Brutus Buckeye's Game Day Rules (Ohio State)

-Wildcat and Scratch's Game Day Rules (Kentucky)

-Rebel's Game Day Rules (Mississippi)

-Willie's Game Day Rules (K-State)

-Big Jay & Baby Jay's Game Day Rules (Kansas)

More to come!
Visit www.GameDayRules.com
for more information.

A Note from the Author

Photo © Sara Hanna Photography - www.SaraHanna.com. The photo was taken at the Swan Coach House.

Sports are more than just a form of exciting entertainment or even a great way to exercise. Sports are a fantastic way to build self-esteem and bring together a sense of community that crosses gender, race, age, economic, social, and even religious lines.

There are many important life lessons that can be learned through sports – how to win AND to lose with grace, being a team player, learning from mistakes, civility towards opposing teams, playing by the rules, respecting the decisions made by the officials – to just name a few. Those skills can be translated into the classroom, the board room, and even in handling the everyday ups and downs of life.

In writing this pledge, it is my goal to instill the solid values of competing with respect, dignity, and integrity in our children, our nation's greatest asset.

-Sherri

SPORTSMANSHIP PLEDGE

LEARN
I will learn how to play the sport, like dribbling and passing the ball.
Learning how to play is great, but having fun is best of all!

EXCELLENCE
I will strive for excellence and live to the best of my best potential.
Doing the best you can is always an essential!

GROWTH
I will exercise my body and the brain in my head.
It is important that they are healthy and that I keep them both well-fed!

INTEGRITY
I will be respectful, honest, and fair, and play according to the rules.
I will behave this way whether at play, at home, or at school!

TEAMWORK
Each member of the team is important, whether coach, player, or me.
I will support them and do my part so we can be the best that we can be!

PLEDGE OF SUPPORT
The Sportsmanship Pledge is an important foundation upon which I will foster and support.
I will be an example and show leadership in this pledge whether on or off the court!